The Little

Spotted Unicorn

By NM Reed

&

McCarthy Preston

Illustrations

by NM Reed

Nejla Shojaie

JD Soriano

Copyright © NM Reed & McCarthy Preston
ISBN: 979-8-9878387-9-2

All rights reserved. No part of this book may be reproduced of transmitted in any form or by
any means, electronic or mechanical, including photocopying,
recording, or by any information storage and retrieval system, without permission in writing
from the copyright owner.

The views expressed in this work are solely those of the author and do not necessarily reflect
the views of the publisher, and the publisher disclaims any
responsibility for them.

Any people depicted in stock imagery provided by any Getty Images
are models, such images are being used for illustrative purposes only. Certain stock imagery
© Getty Images

To order additional copy of this book, contact:
www.littlestcoyote.com www.stevenspressllc.com

The Littlest Coyote and his child were sitting in the sun one day, reading their favorite book

You rarely see Unicorns anymore, they hide where no one would think to look.

They are big and beautiful and shining. By day they hide in the forest in the brightest of sunbeams.

and by night, the owl brought them dreams of their own baby unicorn fawn.

Baby Unicorn fawns were the cutest of all creatures!

The most beautiful of unicorns, Pearl and Splash, were waiting for the birth of their fawn one day when it began to rain.

They saw one of the other unicorns running towards them in the meadow. "Help us, Splash! The babies are caught in the river!" The sky grew dark, and the rain fell.

They ran to the river and saw the babies stranded on a rock way out in the middle. So Splash waded in deep, and called to the baby unicorns, "Here! Jump on my back! Hold on tight!"

When they were safely on his back, Splash swam back to where the others were waiting.

The baby unicorn fawns jumped off his back and were safe. They all thanked Splash. Then the air turned very cold and it started to snow.

The babies were safe, but Splash could not see Pearl anywhere.

He looked high and low. He looked here and there. But Pearl could not be found anywhere.

Just then he saw Pearl, hiding among the trees.
He ran up, he couldn't wait! But what's this?
Her four legs had turned into eight!

Pearl had her new fawn shining and brand new.
Splash could see him standing there in the
cold morning dew.

Pearl cried so loud, "Don't come near, he's all brown with spots, too strange to bear! I saw a little girl and her little dog reading her little book upon a little log. The dog stepped up and touched my face. And all the magic it did erase"

Splash stepped up and said rather strong "Let me look and see what is wrong." He took a look and saw it was strange. It had no horn nor white, and its spots rearranged. "A no-Horn Unicorn! He's beautiful! We'll call him Patches."

The sun came out and the small unicorn family was happy. And Patches the No-Horn unicorn played in the grass.

The night watch owl swooping by overhead when
it was time for them to go to bed

Until one day he grew big and strong, and it was time for him to go on his own.

The herd of wild horses, where all no-horn unicorns go, took him off to their land of rain and snow.

Patches grew up to be the leader of his own herd of no-horn Unicorns.

Sing-along

I wish I were a Unicorn

Oh, I wish I were a Unicorn; that's what I want to be!
A shining long horn of gold, that's what I'd like to see!
Grazing grass and running fast, to frolic in the trees.
My shining long mane of gold, Blowing in the breeze.

I think that I'm a Unicorn, with a gracefully flowing gait.
And with this tail of sparkling gold, now, wouldn't that be great!
I'll use my magic horn of gold to make pure water to drink.
And dance and sing with all my friends, and tell them what I think.

Oh, I feel like I'm a Unicorn, Playing in the sun!
Visiting with all my friends; Saying Hi! To everyone!
They say that we are not for real. But I'll tell you something true.
I think its fact we live inside of every one of you.

But some of you think we're dumb, and hate us, that's for sure!
And for such narrow silliness, there just may be no cure.
But just between you and me, us children old and newer,
We will say with surety you are too mature!

Other Coyote books:

1   The Littlest Coyote
2   The Littlest Coyote Christmas
3   The Littlest Coyote and the Spotted Unicorn
4   The Littlest Coyote and Flowers the Donkey
5   The Littlest Coyote Gets Spring Fever
6   The Littlest Coyote Falls in Love
7   The Littlest Coyote Goes Camping
8   The Littlest Coyote's First Rodeo
9   The Littlest Coyote Saves Rabbit Jack and the Lizard Princess

Available on Amazon.com,
StevensPressLLC.com,
TatteredUnicornPublishing.com,
ETSY.com,
www.LittlestCoyote.com
And social media pages by title, website and author.

Author

NM Reed is an author and illustrator, musician, and entrepreneur living in the mountains of California with dogs, cats, horses and many books. McCarthy Preston is an actor storyteller who directs Role Playing Games at a large Science fiction convention, and holds a mundane career as agent for a large international shipping concern. Nejla Shojaie is an illustrator. She has loved to draw since she was a child. She loves working and living her life as an illustrator and creating children's illustrations. She likes traveling, reading, watching movies and enjoys listening to music, especially when she's drawing.

www.ingramcontent.com/pod-product-compliance
Lightning Source LLC
Chambersburg PA
CBHW041454110726
48007CB00002B/19